W9-DEW-640

and the Heart of a Champion

Books about Cody

Cody and the Fountain of Happiness

Cody and the Mysteries of the Universe

Cody and the Rules of Life

Cody and the Heart of a Champion

CODY

and the Heart of a Champion

TRICIA SPRINGSTUBB

illustrated by
ELIZA WHEELER

CANDLEWICK PRESS

This is a work of fiction. Names, characters, places, and incidents are either products of the author's imagination or, if real, are used fictitiously.

Text copyright © 2018 by Tricia Springstubb
Illustrations copyright © 2018 by Eliza Wheeler

All rights reserved. No part of this book may be reproduced, transmitted, or stored in an information retrieval system in any form or by any means, graphic, electronic, or mechanical, including photocopying, taping, and recording, without prior written permission from the publisher.

First paperback edition 2019

Library of Congress Catalog Card Number 2018940927
ISBN 978-0-7636-7921-7 (hardcover)
ISBN 978-1-5362-0633-3 (paperback)

18 19 20 21 22 23 BVG 10 9 8 7 6 5 4 3 2 1

Printed in Berryville, VA, U.S.A.

This book was typeset in Dante.
The illustrations were done in ink and watercolor.

Candlewick Press
99 Dover Street
Somerville, Massachusetts 02144

visit us at www.candlewick.com

R0454439776

For Linnéa, champion of our hearts
T. S.

For my cousin and first-ever friend, Kristin
E. W.

1
So Confusing

In this life, some things never change:

3 x 3 (always 9)

Ants (always fascinating)

Sauerkraut (always disgusting)

But other things do.

Outside Cody's classroom window, the world was changing before her very eyes. Icicles were melting. Grass was greening. The trees had a happy, fizzy look.

Spring! It was in the air.

Cody loved every season. But if she had to pick, spring would be the grand prize winner.

Good-bye, itchy scarves and annoying hats.

Good-bye, slipping on the ice and landing on your bungie.

Hello, bare feet.

Hello, cartwheels in the grass.

Best of all, her pet ants would un-hibernate. After the long winter, Cody couldn't wait to see them again.

Pearl was tapping her arm. Pearl and Cody ate

lunch together every day. They always tried to be partners. Pearl helped Cody with math, and Cody helped her with . . . well, Pearl didn't need much help. Pearl and Cody were such good friends, they'd even had a sleepover. So far, it was the only sleepover of Cody's life.

Now Pearl looked at her with eyes of guess-what?

"Guess what?" she said. "I'm signing up for soccer."

This was a surprise. Pearl was not what you'd call sporty.

3

"It's super fun," Pearl said. "Plus good exercise. Plus you get to wear cleats. Madison told me all about it when I slept over."

Talk about surprises. Cody looked over at Madison. She was not what you'd call Cody's favorite person. "You had a sleepover with Madison?"

"Twice. It was super fun."

Cody looked down at her math worksheet. How could she still have so many problems left to do?

"Madison says the soccer team has super-fun pizza parties, and everyone gets a trophy."

"Cody and Pearl!" called their teacher, Mr. Daniels. "Are you on task, my friends?"

"Yes, Mr. Daniels!" Quick-quick, Pearl wrote the answers to two of Cody's math problems. Then she whispered, "You should sign up, too."

Madison strolled by on her way to the pencil sharpener.

"Hey, Pearl Girl," she said. "What's kicking?"

Pearl grinned. They bumped fists.

What were cleats? Cody had no idea.

On the way home, Cody unzipped her jacket and pulled off her hat.

"You're jumping the gun," said Spencer, her best friend. "It's still winter. You'll catch a cold."

Winter was over, but it was no use arguing with Spencer. If you enjoyed arguing with a stone wall, you would enjoy arguing with Spencer.

"Pearl wants me to sign up for soccer," she said.

"You'll have to bonk the ball with your bare head." Spencer got a look of pain.

"Pearl says Madison says it's super fun."

"Getting bonked in the head is not fun," said Spencer. "In my experience."

A few days ago, the ground had still been hard and brown. Today, little green nubs poked up. All winter long, the flowers waited in the cold, dark ground.

At last, their patience was being rewarded. Time to come out. Time to bloom. Time for everyone to love them!

"Uh-oh." Spencer pointed across the street. "P.U. alert."

Cody's big brother, Wyatt, was walking with Payton Underwood, the girl of his dreams. Wyatt was a genius, except when P.U. was in the vicinity. Then he went totally mush-brained.

Wyatt and P.U. stopped and stared into each other's eyes. Their faces moved closer. Closer. Slowly, slowly, like a horror movie. P.U. puckered her shiny lips. And then . . .

Cody covered her eyes.

"Tell me when it's over," she whispered.

"Over," Spencer said at last.

When Cody peeked, Wyatt and Payton were holding hands. Wyatt looked like he'd just gotten bonked in the head with a ball. The love ball.

A woman walking by pressed her hand to her heart.

"In spring, a young man's fancy turns to love," she said with a happy sigh.

"What's a fancy?" Cody asked Spencer.

"The opposite of a plain, I guess."

"How about cleats? Do you know what those are?"

"No clue."

Spring was turning out to be a confusing season.

2
Not the Most Important Thing

When Cody walked into the kitchen the next morning, Mom's eyebrows did the Tilt.

"Flip-flops? I don't think so. And those capris are too small."

"No, they're not," said Cody. Even though, to tell the truth, her belly felt a tiny bit pinchy.

"You grew like a weed this winter," Mom said. "You need some new clothes."

The words *new clothes* made Mom go twinkly.

She was Head of Shoes at O'Becker Department Store. A fashion diva, that was Mom. This morning, she wore her navy-blue dress and her high-heeled, red suede boots.

"Do you know what cleats are?" Cody asked.

"They're special athletic shoes." Mom set a bowl of cereal on the table. "Why?"

"Pearl says they're super cool. She wants me to sign up for soccer."

Mom paused. She got a look of how-interesting-is-that!

"Except I don't know how to play," Cody reminded her. "At all."

Mom poured her coffee and let Cody tip in the cream. It made a beautiful swirl, like a galaxy in a cup.

"When I was a girl," said Mom, "I played on a basketball team. We won the city championship three years in a row."

"You never told me that!"

"I still have my medals. The mayor gave them to

us in a special ceremony." Mom got a dreamy look, like she was strolling down Memory Lane. But after a moment she set down her coffee cup. *Clink!* "Of course, winning is not the most important thing."

A tornado hit the kitchen. No, wait. It was Wyatt. Something was going on with his hair. It looked stiff and strange. He grabbed a granola bar.

"Important meeting!" he said as he rushed out the door.

Usually Mom had to drag Wyatt out of bed. Usually he ate six bowls of cereal, at least.

There could only be one explanation.

"Payton Underwood," Mom and Cody said together.

Mom stuck to No Flip-Flops. But she gave Cody permission to wear her spring jacket.

Cody loved that jacket. It was apple red and had six pockets. She found it way in the back of the closet. Like the brave spring flowers, it had waited through the long winter, and now it got its reward.

But something was wrong. Cody couldn't lower her arms. Her elbows stuck out like she was about to do the chicken dance.

"It's too small," said Mom. "You need a new—"

"Bye, Mom! Hope people buy lots of new spring shoes!"

Outside, Cody checked the ant colony. No sign of life yet.

"Hello down there!" she called. "Time to un-hibernate. Here are some cereal crumbs to welcome you."

Spencer was waiting on the corner. His winter jacket was buttoned up to his chin. He wore a hat, scarf, mittens, and boots. Better safe than sorry—that was Spencer's motto.

"Why are you walking like a chicken?" he asked.

"Because. It's fun. Try it."

When they got to school, Pearl cocked her head.

"Why are you walking like two chickens?" she asked.

"Not chickens," Cody said. "Flying squirrels."

"Or vampire bats!" One of Pearl's many talents was her excellent imagination.

That morning, Mr. Daniels opened the classroom windows for the first time. Spicy-sweet outdoor smells drifted in. Cody's toes started to itch. When Mr. Daniels tapped his gong for recess, she ran to line up. Outside, she tugged off her shoes and socks. Ahh. Her feet were happy as prisoners who just got out of jail.

Spring! Whoever named the season was a genius.

Madison ran by, holding a soccer ball. To tell the truth, Cody had always considered Madison kind of wimpy. On the class trip to the Insectarium, she practically fainted at the sight of the giant hissing cockroaches.

Now Madison set the ball on the ground. She cranked her foot. *Ka-pow!* The ball was a blazing rocket.

Wow.

"Isn't she super amazing?" Pearl grabbed Cody's hand. "Come on. Let's play with her."

Pearl started running. Cody stood still.

Rrrip!

"Oh, no!" Pearl got a look of horror. "Was that your jacket?"

It was.

"I'm sorry!" said Pearl. "I didn't mean to rip it."

"I know you didn't." Cody took off the jacket and inspected the hole. She hoped Mom could fix it.

Meanwhile, everyone crowded around Madison. She told them which team they were on, and they obeyed. She was like the Imperial Emperor of Soccer.

"I'm sorry," Pearl said again. Then she grabbed Cody's hand. "Come play! It'll be super fun!"

Before she knew it, Cody was in the middle of the game. Kids stampeded around her. Which way should she look? What was she supposed to do?

"Heads up, Cody!" someone shouted.

Here came the ball! *Kick it,* said her brain. *Ka-pow it!*

Before her foot could get the message, Madison appeared. Her eyes were narrow. Her jaw was set. *Ka-pow!* The ball was gone. Madison streaked after it.

But first she stepped on Cody's bare toes.

Ow! Ow times five!

"Are you all right?" Pearl gasped. "I don't think it's a good idea to play in bare feet."

"I don't think so, either." Cody staggered to the sidelines, where Spencer was watching. "They just keep running back and forth," he said.

"Finally somebody wins."

"Hmm. That means somebody loses."

Clouds slid across the sun. Cody's toes felt cold, as well as flattened.

"You better put your shoes and jacket on." Spencer tugged his hat down. "You'll catch a cold."

Cody pulled her jacket on and shoved her hands into two of the pockets. What was this? An origami frog. Pearl had made it for her last year, as a symbol of friendship.

Now Madison was giving a lesson in how to bonk the ball with your head. Pearl listened with a face of concentration. She seemed to have forgotten all about Cody's ripped jacket and squished toes.

Cody looked down at the paper frog. It was crumpled and old, like something from a museum. Like something from long-ago times.

That night, Mom brought home presents.

Wyatt got a new shirt. It had buttons and a collar, exactly the kind of shirt he hated. Wyatt was a T-shirt person. His favorites had pictures of exploding aliens. Or the digestive system. (Wyatt was going to be a doctor.)

But in this life, many things are hard to predict. Including people who are gaga in love.

"Payton likes collars," Mom whispered to Cody. "Also, apparently, hair product."

Cody's present was a pair of orange shoes with zebra stripes. The bottoms had bumps.

"They're cleats," said Mom. "See if they fit."

Of course they did. Perfectly. If anyone knew feet, it was Mom. *Clomp-clomp.*

"Cody's going to try her hand at soccer," Mom told Wyatt.

"Her foot, you mean. No hands allowed in soccer."

Wyatt put on his shirt. Gazing in the mirror, he smiled at his new, stiff-haired, buttoned-up self. For about five seconds. Then he stuck his finger inside the collar and tugged. He made a face of I-am-being-strangled-to-death.

Tug-tug. Clomp-clomp.

3
True Grit

Soccer sign-up was on Saturday. Cody *clomp-clomped* into the kitchen. And sneezed.

"Uh-oh." Dad held up his spatula, like a crossing guard with a STOP sign. "Somebody's got the sniffles."

Cody blew her nose and sat down. Dad served her a stack of his special secret-ingredient pancakes. Dad was a trucker. He drove a big rig and was on the road a lot. Whenever he came home, he made pancakes.

The yummiest pancakes ever. The secret ingredient was: Dad was home.

A-choo! She sneezed again.

"Do you feel okay? Maybe we should skip the sign-ups."

Outside, the sky had an unfriendly look. Up in the tree, the birds puffed their feathers into tiny puffer coats. Where had spring gone?

"It's a good day for staying inside and playing crazy eights," said Dad.

That sounded so nice. But Pearl said Cody *had* to come. Otherwise they might not be on the same team.

"I'm fine," she told her father.

She put her dish in the sink, then pulled on her apple-red jacket. She kept forgetting to ask Mom to fix it, and the hole was even bigger now.

Another good thing about Dad: he didn't really notice what you wore, as long as you weren't naked.

Outside, the wind growled and bit their noses.

"Woo-eee," said Dad. "That wind is fierce!"

Before she got in the car, Cody checked on the ants. Nope. She heaved a sigh. Who could blame them? She'd rather be snuggled in a cozy nest, too.

Sign-up was at the middle school. The parking lot was jammed. Inside, parents filled out forms while kids cleat-clomped around. Pearl came running over.

"You're just in time! We're having a scrimmage."

The word sounded familiar. Was it some kind of snack? After all those pancakes, Cody wasn't really hungry. But Dad said go ahead, so Cody followed Pearl outside. Millions of kids were running around kicking balls.

A man with a clipboard wrote down Cody's name. Pearl pulled a yellow vest over Cody's head. She had one, too.

"We have to try to play just like Madison," Pearl said.

Now that she had official cleats instead of bare

feet, Cody was ready. She'd always been a fast runner, and now she ran like an Australian tiger beetle, which is the fastest insect on earth.

Up and down, back and forth. She scrimmaged away. Her nose ran, but she wiped it on her sleeve. Her tummy spun, but she paid no attention. Nothing could stop her.

"You're doing great," shouted Pearl as she ran by. "Only, try to get the ball sometimes."

Okay. Cody could do that, too.

Maybe not, said the stack of special pancakes inside her.

Greenish, that was how she suddenly felt. But she couldn't stop now. She had to be good enough to get on Pearl's team.

Just then, three girls tried to get the ball at once. Their legs tangled up and they fell down in a heap. The ball rolled away.

Here was Cody's chance. She cranked her leg the

way she'd seen Madison do. *Wham!* The ball was jet-propelled! Cody watched with eyes of astonishment.

And then she turned and ran some more, this time toward the bathroom. *Here we come,* her pancakes were saying, *ready or not.*

"You were amazing," Pearl told her later on the phone. "So what if you kicked the ball the wrong direction? It takes true grit to play till you barf."

"Tanks." By now Cody's nose was all stuffed up. Dad had made her cambric tea, like they drank in *Little House on the Prairie.*

"You have the heart of a champion," said Pearl.

Pearl was one of the nicest people on the entire planet. In the solar system. In the galaxy. In the universe. Which Wyatt said was getting bigger by the second.

"I hope we're on the same team," Cody said. "We can be the Deadly Duo."

"Don't forget Madison. We'll be the Terrible Trio!"

Cody sniffled. "Oday."

• • •

"How was soccer?" Spencer asked the next day.

Cody shrugged. She didn't feel like talking about puking.

Spencer lived in a side-by-side. On the other side lived the Meen family. Thank goodness they weren't home.

The porch swing swung, even though no one sat in it. You could practically hear the wind bragging. *I am fieeeeerce! Fieeeeeerce, I say!*

"Let's go inside," said Cody. "I'll help you all make dinner."

Sunday dinner was an important event at Spencer's house. He, his parents, and his grandmother GG all lived together, and they always made a big feast.

"My parents had to go somewhere." Spencer took off his glasses. Without them, he looked kind of breakable.

"Where'd they go?"

"My mom is having a baby."

"Right now?" This seemed sudden.

"In September." He did some nervous blinking.

"Wow. Is it a boy or a girl?"

"They don't know." More blinking. "They want it to be a surprise."

Spencer was not big in the surprise department. Every morning he ate the exact same thing for breakfast. Hooley's peanut butter on toast. When his family went on vacation, they took along a jar of Hooley's. Every night, he kissed his mother first. Then his father. Then GG. If one of them wasn't home, Spencer had a hard time going to sleep.

Also, he did not like loud noises, throw-up, or the smell of poop.

A baby was really going to throw things off track.

He put his glasses back on, but he still looked thin around the edges.

"It will be okay," Cody said. These were feel-better words. She hoped they were true words, too.

"I don't want to talk about it." He lifted his chin. "Anyway, I'm making a museum."

It was under the front porch. You might think what a strange place for precious, museum-y objects, but not if you knew Spencer. He had dusted away the cobwebs. He had spread out an old, clean rug.

The only problem was, the museum had nothing in it.

"What kind of museum is it?" she asked.

"A special kind."

Cody sneezed. Spencer could have said, *I told you you'd get a cold*. But he was not an I-told-you-

so type. Instead, he crawled out to get her some tissues.

Cody waited. Someone climbed the front steps. *Stomp-stomp!* It must be Mr. Meen, who killed bugs for a living and wore heavy steel-toed boots. *Stomp-stomp!* Cody tried not to giggle. He'd never guess she was under here!

Spencer came back with tissues, a blanket, a thermos of cocoa, two mugs, marshmallows, and MewMew, GG's old, adorable deaf cat. The blanket

felt wonderful. MewMew thought so, too. She snuggled in Cody's lap and began to purr.

Spencer poured the cocoa. He'd even put in marshmallows, Cody's number-one food. The three of them sat, peacefully sipping and purring.

"I think this should be a clubhouse instead of a museum," Cody said.

Remember about arguing with Spencer? Like arguing with a stone wall?

"Okay," she said at last. "It's a museum. I'll make the signs that tell what things are. And why they're amazing."

"That would be good," said Spencer. "That would be very good, in my opinion."

The wind huffed and puffed, but it couldn't get them under the porch. Under the porch, nobody could see them. All the rest of the world seemed far, far away.

Maybe this was how it felt to be an ant, snug and hibernating underground with your best buddies.

4
Epic!

As much as Spencer hated surprises, that was how much Cody loved them. But even for a surprise lover, three in one night was a bit much.

Surprise #1: When Cody got home, Payton Underwood was sitting on the living-room couch. So were Wyatt and Mom. They were watching basketball.

"Did you see that fadeaway?" cried Payton. "Is LeBron insanely good or what?"

"Insanely," said Mom.

"I'm such a fan."

"Me too."

Mom and Payton reached over Wyatt's head and high-fived. Wyatt looked confused. He scratched his stiff-as-glue head. He tugged his collar.

Strange. Strange times three.

Surprise #2: Dad had news.

"Pearl called. She said you're on the same team with her and . . . was it Jefferson?" He wiped his hands on his apron and gave her a hug. "Congratulations, Little Seed! Looks like you're a soccer player."

Surprise #3: Mom wouldn't fix her apple-red jacket.

"It's too small. You need a new one."

"No, I don't. I need this one."

"The store just got in some darling reversible jackets. I'll bring you one."

Cody's nose itched. Her eyes prickled. Her evil cold was taking over her entire body. Out of the blue, she felt tired and used up. Like an old jacket. A jacket that once was new but got tossed in a scrap heap. Never to be worn or loved again. That made her so sad, tears spurted into her eyes.

"Oh, honey." Mom pulled her close. Cody breathed in her mother's wonderful perfume, which was called Love Potion Number Nine. "All right. I'll fix it. But I'm warning you, it will only rip again."

No, it wouldn't. Because Cody was going to be extra, extra, super-duper careful.

The next morning, the tree outside her window *tap-tapped* on the glass. This was tree for "Help! Winter has me back in its clutches!"

Cody trudged into the kitchen. Sweet Mom had kept her promise and mended the jacket. But Mean Mom said it was too cold to wear it.

It was freezing out. *Ha-ha!* cackled winter. *I, evil winter, rule the world!*

Cody left her toast crusts for the ants. Just in case.

On the walk to school, Spencer was unnaturally

quiet. Cody asked if he found out what kind of baby it was. He shook his head. She asked if he'd tell her what kind of museum it was. More head shaking. She asked if something was wrong. Spencer hesitated. His chin went up. Then it went sideways. Then back down.

"Is that a yes or a no?" Cody asked.

Before he could make up his mind, Pearl and Madison raced toward them.

"Teammates! Teammates!" They grabbed Cody's hands and started jumping up and down.

"This is going to be epic!" said Madison. "Last year, the grown-ups said it was a tie, no matter what. But this year, they'll keep real score. Somebody will *win*. And guess who it will be?"

"Who?" asked Cody.

"Duh!" said Madison. "Us!"

"We'll be nice to the losers, though," said Pearl.

They all did more jumping up and down. Cody's hat popped off and Spencer picked it up for her.

• • •

Spencer's parents worked at home, and they kid-sat Cody after school. This afternoon, the Meen kids, Molly and Maxie, were in the backyard. The Meens often lived up to their name. But not always. In this life, some people keep you on your toes.

Molly and Maxie were busy dragging chairs out into the backyard.

"What are you doing?" asked Spencer.

"What does it look like?" said Molly.

It looked like they were putting kitchen chairs all over the yard.

"They're hurt-alls," said her little sister.

"Hurdles," corrected Molly. She crouched down. "Runners, take your marks." She tilted forward. "Set." She shot her finger in the air. "Bang!"

She was off. When she came to a chair, she threw one leg out and sailed over. Wow. It looked impossible and easy at the same time. After the last chair, Molly pumped her fists.

"Two, four, seven, eight!" cheered Maxie. "Molly Meen is really great!"

"I'm training to be an Olympic track star," Molly said.

"I'm training to be a cheerleader," Maxie said.

While Molly practiced hurdling, Cody tried to teach Maxie to do a cartwheel. In this life, you never know how complicated something is till you try to teach somebody else.

By the time Cody looked around for Spencer, he had disappeared. She went inside to find him.

The kitchen was a disaster zone. An avalanche of dishes, cups, papers, books, and LEGOs buried everything. Spencer's father, Mr. Pickett, stood by the sink. He was using a cutting board for a desk.

In the dining room, Mrs. Pickett was typing and talking into a headset. She looked the same as ever. Could she really have a baby inside? It must be like the spring flowers and the ants, patiently waiting inside the earth.

Stepping over toys and shoes and MewMew, Cody went to the front door and out on the porch. Nobody.

"Down here," said a voice from below.

Cody jumped down the steps. She crawled into the museum.

"It's okay if you're not good at sports," she told Spencer. "You don't have to feel bad."

"I don't feel bad," he said. "I just wanted to get to work here."

He pointed at a tube of paper lying on the rug.

"Could you help me hang this up?"

The tube looked strangely familiar. As Cody unrolled it, she knew why.

"It's the WELCOME SPENCER banner from when you moved here!" She and GG had made it together. GG had written the words, and Cody had drawn the ants. "I didn't know you kept it all this time."

It took a gazillion pieces of tape to stick it to the wall, but at last the banner was up. They gazed at it with eyes of pride.

"Maybe we should cross out SPENCER and write TO THE MUSEUM instead," Cody suggested.

Spencer shook his round head. Fine. Using a crayon and an index card, Cody made this label:

Offishull Welcome Spencer banner. Made by Grandma Grace and Cody. Notiss friendly ants.

It must be an art museum, she thought.

"*¿Hola?*" called a voice. "*¿Mi hermana?*"

Cody crawled back out. There stood Wyatt.

And Payton.

That pesky girl was everywhere these days. She pulled out her lip gloss and smeared some on.

"Is this your secret clubhouse?" she asked.

"It's not a clubhouse," Cody said. "Besides, how could it be secret if you know about it?"

Payton laughed. "You are crazy smart," she said. "Just like your big brother." She gazed up at Wyatt with eyes of you-are-so-the-one.

Mush. You could practically see it leaking out Wyatt's ears.

5
Surprise City

Mom bought Cody shiny orange shorts and long orange socks to match her cleats.

"Do I look like a Creamsicle?" Cody asked Pearl as they rode to practice.

"You look epic!"

Pearl's mother was driving them. Cody sat in back, between the twins in their car seats. Her tummy was full of butterflies. Or dragonflies. Or flying cockroaches.

Good thing she didn't eat any pancakes.

When they got out of the car, the twins called, "Bye-bye, sistaw!" They waved their sippy cups.

"Being a baby is so easy," said Cody. "All you have to do is eat, sleep, and play."

"Tell me about it," said Pearl. "But they don't get to play soccer like us!"

Their coach's name was Yazmin. She wore a whistle and a sweatshirt that said COACH Y! She told them each to get a ball and practice dribbling.

Cody laughed. Dribbling was what the twins did when they drank from their sippy cups! But what do you know? *Dribble* also meant "kick the ball a little at a time."

Surprise City. That was soccer.

Ball dribbling was harder than it looked. Cody and Pearl could not get the hang of it. The ball went wherever it wanted.

"Cody, are you left- or right-handed?" Coach Y! asked.

"I'm training to be ambidextrous. But I'm still mostly left-handed."

"I knew it. You're probably left-footed. Switch feet and try."

Whoa. That was easier. Now the coach coached Pearl. For a long time. Somehow Pearl couldn't get the hang of things.

Another soccer surprise. Pearl was usually excellent at everything.

Time for drills. The drills had names like Keep Your Yard Clean and Knock Out. The team kicked and ran, ran and kicked. Cody's legs felt like those old rubber bands you find in the back of a drawer. Her nose began to itch. Uh-oh. Here came a sneeze. The enormous, squinch-your-eyes kind.

A-choo!

Whomp!

She crashed into Madison. They both toppled to the ground.

"I'm sorry!" Cody said. "Are you okay?"

"Forget it." Madison did a snort. "That was nothing. I've been knocked down ten times harder than that."

"You have?"

"Soccer is not for weaklings," said Madison.

When Pearl's mother came to pick them up, the twins were in their jammies. They smelled like powder and lotion. And like the bananas they were smushing all over everything.

"Cody was epic," Pearl told her mother. "Way better than me."

"I was not," said Cody.

"Was so."

"Not."

"So."

"Not."

"So."

The twins thought this was hilarious. They kicked their jammie feet. They waved their bananas around like mushy swords.

"Is that banana in your hair?" Mom asked at dinner.

Cody was too tired to explain.

After they cleared the table, she followed Wyatt into his room. Gremlin came, too. Gremlin used to belong to Wyatt and still enjoyed visiting him. He and Cody rested their heads on Wyatt's pillow, which smelled like anti-pimple soap. It was interesting how a smell could be disgusting but you still liked it because it was the smell of someone you loved.

Wyatt had whipped off his collar shirt as soon as he got home from school. In his ancient, holey T-shirt, he looked much more Wyatt-ish.

"Guess what?" she said. "I'm left-footed."

"Awesome," he said. "That's a recessive gene."

When Wyatt's brain wasn't turned to mush, it was wall-to-wall information. It was an information storehouse in there.

Bidda-la-beep went his phone. A text. Then another one. And another one. If you are wondering who was sending them, you have not been paying very good attention.

"Payton is an epic pest these days," said Cody.

"That's because we're officially boyfriend and girlfriend."

"You are?" Cody sat up.

"Payton decided she's mature enough for a committed relationship," he said.

Cody wasn't sure what *mature* meant, but it sounded dangerous. Wyatt's face was hard to figure out. It reminded Cody of the man in the moon. Beaming. But also kind of worried.

Bidda-la-beep!

"I'll never get my chemistry done."

He ran a hand over his hair. It did not move. Even outside, in the fierce bully wind, his hair did not move. "Plus I have a killer math test tomorrow."

"Give me the phone. I'll text her for you."

"Very funny."

A-choo!

"Hey, cover that sneeze, please."

"I hate this cold." Cody flopped back down. "Spencer warned me not to take off my jacket."

"You don't get a cold from taking off your jacket. You have to come in contact with a highly contagious rhinovirus."

Bidda-la-beep!

Cody wondered if a rhinovirus had a tusk. And little beady eyes. Wyatt would know, but he had to study. And keep answering all those texts. Still, she had one more thing to tell him.

"Madison said soccer is not for weaklings."

"No problema," said Wyatt. "The last thing you are is a weakling."

Cody wanted to hug her brother. But she knew he'd put her in a Houdini headlock, so she hugged Gremlin instead.

Bidda-la-beep!

6
Fierce

First thing every day, Cody checked on the ants. She called, "Hello? Hello down there?" She sang "You Are My Sunshine." She put her ear to the ground and listened for activity.

All was still. All was silent.

Every morning, she left some crumbs, in case today was the day. But she was starting to get worried about her underground friends.

• • •

"I have violin tomorrow morning," Spencer said on Friday. "So I'm going to work on the museum in the afternoon."

"But I have a soccer game in the afternoon!"

"Our schedules conflict. That happens to my parents all the time."

"We can work on it after church on Sunday."

"I don't know." *Blink-blink* went Spencer's eyes. "I might be busy."

"Busy with what?"

"The baby. We have to get ready."

What did they have to get ready? Babies needed a lot of diapers, Cody knew that. But how long would it take to buy diapers?

"My mother keeps puking," Spencer said.

Nobody likes puking. But Spencer was especially sensitive. Once, a girl in his class threw up on his shoes and he had to go home, too, because he was so upset.

"Just the smell of food turns her green. MewMew

has to eat down in the basement, because cat food sends her right over the edge."

Poor MewMew. Poor Mrs. Pickett. This baby wasn't even born, and it was already changing everything.

Cody's soccer jersey was red and black. Her number was 6. Not one of her favorites, but you didn't get to choose.

Before the game, Coach Y! called a huddle.

"I'm proud of how hard you've worked in practice," she told the team. "Try to remember what you've learned. Focus. Communicate. Most of all, remember our motto. What's our motto?"

"*We*, not *me!*" they yelled.

Dad was on the road, but Mom was there. Even though Saturday was the busiest day at O'Becker, she had taken off. That made Cody happy. Also a little nervous. What if their team was no good? What if Mom wasted her precious time off for nothing?

"I hope we win," Cody told Pearl as they put on their shin guards.

"Winning is not the most important thing," said Pearl.

"I know. But it's pretty important."

"I wish I was half as good as Madison."

"Me too. I wish we were both star players."

"I can't even dribble right."

"Just try your best."

Pearl's nose wrinkled. *A-choo!*

"Are we ready, team?" cried Coach Y!

Madison was a striker. Pearl was a defender. Cody was a midfielder. They each had different jobs to do, though Cody wasn't so exactly 100 percent sure about it all.

Kickoff!

Playing soccer was a lot like sneezing. It set your brain on *blink*. All you could think about was *Right this second*. Run this way, run that way, try for the ball, miss the ball, run some more. All around you, everyone was doing the same thing, except when the referee blew the whistle, which, thank goodness, meant "Stop and catch your breath."

At halftime, they chewed on oranges. The coach said they were doing fantastic.

"Not!" Madison shook her head. She made eyes of disaster. "We're down by one!"

"Easy does it." Coach Y! put a hand on her shoulder. "Let's just play our game."

After halftime, the teams changed sides. Cody remembered to run the opposite way. She remembered to dribble with her left foot. She remembered to pass only to people on her own team.

On the sidelines, Mom cheered. "Good job, number six! That's the way!"

Cody waved at her. Mom waved back. Everybody started yelling. For a tiny second, Cody thought they were cheering for her. Which felt so nice! But then she realized. Madison had just scored. The game was tied!

The coach took out Cody and Pearl and sent in two other girls. Cody and Pearl sucked their water bottles.

"It's all up to Madison," said Pearl.

Cody was surprised. "That's not what the coach says. She says it's up to us all together."

Pearl sneezed but did not take her eyes off the field.

"Madison is our only chance," she said.

That was when everybody started yelling again. Madison had the ball! She charged down the field, zeroing in on the net. The goalie darted back and forth, waving her giant gloves. Madison zigged. She zagged. Her eyes were narrow. Her jaw was set. There was no stopping her!

"She's going to score!" yelled Pearl. "We're going to win!"

The goalie waved her monster gloves.

Madison tilted sideways.

Uh-oh! She was going to fall.

No, she wasn't! She was back on her feet.

Cranking her foot. Taking her shot. *Ka-pow!* The ball zooped over the goalie's head and into the net.

Just as the referee blew his whistle.

"We won!" Cody and Pearl hugged. "We won!"

So why didn't the coach look happy? Why did Madison fold her arms and stamp her cleats?

Because the game was over, and it was a tie after all. After they did high fives with the other team, Coach Yazmin called a huddle. She explained that the ref had ruled a hand ball. Madison had touched the ball, so her goal didn't count.

"I didn't really touch it!" cried Madison. "Just one tiny fingertip! Maybe two."

"I know you're disappointed, Mad," said the coach.

Disappointed-mad. Cody knew how that felt.

"It's not fair." Madison's bottom lip trembled. "That ref is mean. It was an accident."

"At least we didn't lose," Pearl said in a voice of helpfulness.

"A tie is as bad as losing!" Madison grabbed her bag and ran to where her father waited. When he put his arm around her, she buried her head in his chest.

Cody hated when people cried. Even if they cried

over something she would never cry over, she still hated it.

That night, Dad called from the road. While Cody waited her turn to talk, she checked the sofa cushions for interesting things. Whoa! One of Payton's lip glosses.

"How was the game?" Dad asked.

"It was a tie."

"In the game of life, you can do way worse than a tie."

Cody pulled the top off the lip gloss. It smelled like one of those delicious artificial drinks Mom didn't let them have.

"Madison says a tie is as bad as losing," she told Dad.

"Who's Madison?"

Cody told how, on their class field trip to the Insectarium, Madison almost fainted over the Madagascar hissing cockroaches.

"She's a cute-animal kind of girl," Cody said. "She likes koalas."

"Koalas and soccer."

"She doesn't just *like* soccer. She's . . ." Cody remembered Madison's face as she raced down the field. "She's *fierce* about it."

"Well," said Dad, "it's good to be fierce about something. It's good to really care about something, and give it all you've got."

This was so confusing. What about *Winning isn't the most important thing*? And *It's how you play the game that matters*?

Cody sniffed the lip gloss again. It smelled delicious. It smelled so good, you could almost take a bite out of it.

Oops.

7
Soccer Land

As she walked to Spencer's house the next day, Cody wondered about all the people she saw. Was that old man sweeping his driveway fierce about something? How about that woman balancing a big white cake box in her arms? Could little kids whose bikes still had training wheels be fierce?

At Spencer's, MewMew sat looking out the front window. She tapped the glass with her paw. This was cat for "I am thrilled to see you!" Then she yawned and curled up for a nap.

MewMew was fierce about naps.

The door on the other side of the porch opened. Out came Maxie Meen, waving blue pom-poms.

"GG's at church. A lady in a big car came and picked up the rest of them."

Cody remembered what Spencer said about getting ready for the baby. Did the lady take them to buy diapers? That didn't make sense.

Maxie stood on her tiptoes. "What's on your mouth?" she asked.

"Lip gloss."

"Can I have some?"

Cody dabbed some on her finger and rubbed it on Maxie's mouth. She licked her lips like a little cat.

In the backyard, Molly was hurdling over cardboard boxes. Mr. Meen had put the kibosh on dragging furniture outside. Cody helped Maxie practice cartwheels.

"Go with the flow," she said. That was what GG said when they did tai chi together. "Experience harmony. Become one with the windmill."

Half a century went by. Still no Spencer.

At last Cody gave up. She decided to visit the museum before she went home.

What do you know? Spencer had added a new exhibit. It was the catapult they'd built last summer. Cody smiled as she remembered how much fun they'd had smithereening eggs. That was the day she and Spencer became best friends for life.

Cody hoped you spelled *catapult* the way it sounded. On an index card she wrote:

Egg catapullt. Made by Cody and Spencer. Very usefull.

She taped on the sign. It looked professional, if she did say so herself.

Maybe this wasn't an art museum after all. But then, what kind of museum could it be?

The evil, creeping rhinovirus got hold of Pearl next.

She had a special technique of coughing into her elbow so she wouldn't spread germs. Also, she carried a giant bottle of hand sanitizer everywhere. Including to lunch, where they were going now.

"We have to sit at the soccer table," she told Cody.

Cody imagined a table shaped like a soccer ball. That cracked her up! Everything would slide off.

But when they got to the lunchroom, she saw what Pearl meant. All the soccer kids were sitting together. Cody waved to Spencer, who was unwrapping his sandwich at another table. He came to sit with them.

Spencer's head swiveled back and forth as people talked about soccer camp. And soccer travel teams. And their favorite soccer pros. It was Soccer Land, all right. In Cody's opinion, the conversation needed a little pick-me-up.

"Did anybody watch that show about beetles?" she asked. "They showed one so strong, it can snap a pencil in half."

"Bugs totally creep me out!" said Madison. She pushed away her chicken nuggets. "Now I can't eat."

That was silly.

"Cody didn't mean it." Pearl pumped sanitizer. "It's just that she loves . . ." She hesitated. "She loves B-U-G-S."

"Eee-yoo!" Madison covered her eyes. "I might upchuck."

Spencer got up and moved to the other end of the table.

"Tell her you're sorry," whispered Pearl, rubbing her sanitized hands together. "Tell her you didn't mean it."

Cody didn't mean to make Madison upset. But she did mean that a pencil-snapping beetle was as interesting as S-O-C-C-E-R. To her, at least.

"Tell her!" Pearl suddenly spoke in a voice of command.

Whoa. Sometimes Pearl talked that way to the juice-dribbling, banana-mushing twins. But never, ever to Cody. Cody was so startled, she dropped a tater tot into her chocolate pudding.

"I'm sorry," said Cody.

"Please don't do it again," said Madison.

"She won't," said Pearl.

"It's called a Hercules beetle," whispered Cody, so quietly no one heard.

"Are you going to sit with them every day?" Spencer asked on the way home.

"Pearl says it's part of being a team."

"I didn't under-stand anything they said. They might as well have been speaking Norwegian."

Cody laughed. The warm weather had made a comeback, and she'd put her flip-flops in her backpack. Now she slipped them on. Her escaped toes wiggled for joy.

But then she remembered something.

"Where were you yesterday?"

"Be careful." Spencer pointed at her feet. "Flip-flops don't offer good support."

That is called changing the subject.

"I waited and waited for you. How many diapers does one baby need?"

"Diapers?" Spencer took off his woolly hat. He scratched his round head. "What are you talking about?"

"Fine. Don't tell me." Cody marched away. But not very far. Because she tripped. And landed on her bungie.

Did Spencer say *I told you so*? Or did he kindly help her up?

You probably know the answer by now.

"I like the sign you made for our catapult," he said.

"Remember that day? That was when we became best friends for life."

Spencer smiled. But quick-quick, the smile vanished.

This was suspicious behavior. What was going on here?

"Spencer, are you ready to tell me what kind of museum it is?"

He pulled his hat back on and shook his head.

Fine. Cody would wait.

Número uno, with Spencer you didn't really have a choice.

Número dos, with Spencer waiting was always worth it.

8
Empty House

Mr. Daniels tapped the little gong on his desk. *Gonggg!* Journal Time.

Today they had to write about Something I Am Looking Forward To. *Spring.* The word sprang into Cody's head. She picked up her pencil.

"Do you need help spelling *tournament?*" Pearl asked her.

"Huh?"

"The big soccer tournament? Coming up next week?"

"Oh." Cody chewed her eraser. "Right."

"You didn't forget about it, did you?"

"I remember." Well, now she did.

"Cody and Pearl," called Mr. Daniels. "On task, my friends."

They bent over their journals.

"It's going to be wicked exciting," Pearl whispered. "You play till you get eliminated. No ties allowed. If it's a tie, they do sudden death."

Cody imagined her whole team falling over, suddenly dead. She grabbed Pearl's sanitizer and pumped a big gob.

That was when Pearl did something completely un-Pearl. She nibbled her eraser. Cody was the pencil chewer, not Pearl.

"Madison says my dribbling is still weak," said Pearl.

"I think your dribbling is great."

"Not."

"Is."

"Not."

"Is."

"Cody and Pearl!" Their teacher ran a hand over his cowlick. "Is there a problem?"

"No, Mr. Daniels!"

Pearl nibbled her slimy eraser. Cody began to get a strange feeling. A feeling that Pearl was changing, right before her eyes. She was falling under the spell of Madison.

"Cody, why are you looking at me like that?"

"Pearl, are you fierce about soccer?"

"Fierce?" Pearl drew back. "I don't think so. Predators are fierce. I am a peaceful person." She held up two fingers for the peace sign.

That made Cody feel better. Bending over her journal, she wrote

I am looking forward to spring. It is my best season. In spring things that went away come back. For exampull ants. And flowers. Brand new things come. For exampull baby birds. And baby people.

Gonggg! Lunchtime.

On the way, she and Pearl made peace signs at everyone. In the lunchroom, Cody tried to sit down, but Madison held up her hand. She pulled out a chart and consulted it.

"Today is Pearl's day to sit on my left side, and Gopal's day to sit on my right. You don't get to sit next to me till, umm, Thursday."

"Madison's just trying to be fair," explained Pearl. "Everyone wants to sit by her. This way we all get our turn."

Cody moved to the end of the table. So what? Who cared? She'd sit with Spencer. Her trusty, true best friend for life. He'd be here any minute.

No, he wouldn't.

"Where were you?" she asked him on the way home. This was a question she was asking him an awful lot lately.

"You don't have to get upset."

73

"I'm not upset!" Cody yelled.

"The Spindle said I could eat in our room. I helped her fold programs for the spring concert."

The Spindle was Spencer's teacher. The two had a lot in common. They both loved music and sturdy, sensible shoes.

"That sounds like the boring-est thing on earth," Cody said, but Spencer shrugged.

"Eating at the soccer table is boring. In my experience."

"Ha," said Cody. *Ha* can mean "That's funny." Or "That's crazy." Or "Exactly!" It is a very useful word when you are not at all sure what you mean.

That night, Mom brought Wyatt another button-up shirt.

"You can't keep wearing the same one every day," she said.

Wyatt took one look and wrapped his hands around his neck.

"Do you have a sore throat?" Mom felt his forehead.

"He has the love disease," said Cody.

Bidda-la-beep! went his phone, and he hurried out of the room.

Mom had brought Cody something, too. A new jacket.

"Look. It's reversible!"

Mom demonstrated. One minute, the jacket was midnight blue. The next, it was forest green with midnight-blue cats. A two-for-one jacket!

"Look," said Mom. "It even has a secret pocket."

Cody tried it on. She could lift her arms up high. No more chicken

dance. Deluxe, that was the only way to describe this new jacket.

But what about her old one? It had been her favorite for so long. How could she just abandon it? Was that any way to treat a trusty friend?

Cody thanked Mom, then hung the jacket up. She put on her old mended one and went outside. It was almost dark. The spring flowers had folded up into little yellow and purple fists. Somewhere, somebody's dog gave a lonesome bark.

"I'm getting pretty worried," she whispered to the ants. "Is everything okay down there?"

She *knock-knocked* on the ground. It felt like knocking on the door of an empty house.

For days, a terrible thought had been hiding in a corner of her brain. Now it poked its head out. What if the ants had moved? What if their colony got too crowded? Or what if they got bored and wanted a change of scenery?

What if they had packed up and left?

The dog gave another lonesome bark.

Quick-quick, Cody tried to stand up. Instead, she lost her balance and fell over backward.

R-r-rip!

9
Bossy Boss

Mother Nature had lost her mind. In the morning, fat white snowflakes filled the air. Even the snowflakes looked confused. They swirled this way and that. You could almost hear them asking, *Does anybody know the plan?*

That afternoon, Cody and Spencer went to his house. Whatever is the opposite of neat as a pin, that was Spencer's house. Where would they ever fit the new baby? On top of the refrigerator, maybe?

Mrs. Pickett tried to fix their snack. But when she

opened the pizza box, her face turned an unearthly color. She sprinted out of the kitchen. They had to microwave it themselves.

Spencer cut his pizza with a knife. Yes, he really did this.

"My parents say babies don't know anything. If a baby was a computer, it wouldn't have any downloads. I'll have to teach it everything."

This sounded good to Cody. She liked being in charge.

"But I don't know *every*thing!" said Spencer.

"You know how to play the violin. And make amazing LEGOs. And do check-plus school projects."

Spencer did not look convinced.

"I can help you." Cody fed MewMew some pepperoni. "And Wyatt has lots of big brother experience. He can be your coach. Coach W!"

Spencer slid his eyes to the left. Then to the right. Sneaky, that was how he looked. Before Cody could ask what exactly was going on, he jumped up.

"I have a new museum exhibit," he said.

He went to his room and came back with an origami dinosaur.

"Remember?" he said. "Pearl made it for me last year. It's an allosaurus."

Of course Cody remembered. Her heart did a dip, remembering those happy days of old.

"You kept it all this time, and it's still like new," she said.

They looked up how to spell *origami* and *allosaurus* in the dictionary. On a card she wrote:

Origami allosaurus, made long ago by our friend Pearl. Real dino was much bigger.

They set it next to the catapult. Sitting side by side on the rug, they admired the exhibits.

"I think you're going to be a wonderful big brother," Cody said. "Know why?"

"Why?"

"Because you're really, really good at taking care of things."

Spencer smiled. They touched foreheads and did a little rub-a-dub-dub. This was how friendly ants greeted one another, and it was their special secret sign.

That night, Mother Nature came to her senses. By morning, all the snow had melted.

On the ride to soccer practice, the twins fussed and whined and blew snot rockets. They were the latest victims of the rhinovirus. Squished between them, Cody tried to cheer them up with a riddle.

"What goes up but doesn't come down? Give up? Your age!"

The twins didn't get it. One started crying. Uh-oh. Those two did everything together. Cody stuck her fingers in her ears. By the time they got to soccer practice, she wasn't sure if she'd ever be able to hear again.

Coach Y! had them do passing drills. Cody and Madison were partners.

"Here you go!" Cody passed her the ball.

Focus was Madison's middle name. She focused so hard, she forgot to pass the ball back to Cody. Instead she ran all the way down the field and shot it into the net.

"Gooooooal!" yelled Cody. She and Madison fist-bumped.

But Coach Y! planted her hands on her hips.

"Passing means two people," she said. "No ball hogs on this team."

Ball hogs! Cody pictured a pen full of balls, like at Playland, only with pigs instead of kids rolling around. She tried not to laugh. Coach Y! was fierce about teamwork.

Cody and Madison tried again.

"Pass!" yelled Madison. "Over here! Not like that! Watch how I do it! Inside of your foot! Not so hard! Try again, Cody!"

Whew.

Meanwhile, Pearl practiced her dribble. She still

could not get the hang of it. Miserable, that was the face of Pearl.

"You're getting better," Cody told her.

"Do you think so?"

"Do bears poop in the woods?"

Usually, this made Pearl giggle. But not today.

Their coach explained that the tournament would be a new and challenging experience. They'd learn more about teamwork. And stamina, which meant never giving up. A tournament was the chance to play many different teams.

"If we don't get eliminated." Madison made eyes of darkness.

"All together," said their coach.

"*WE, NOT ME!*"

On the way home, the twins were asleep. Cody leaned toward the front seat.

"Madison is bossy," she whispered.

Pearl never called names. She bit her lip. Her forehead wrinkled.

"I wouldn't use that word."

"I would," said Cody. "Bossy bossy."

"She doesn't mean to be. She just wants us all to be the best we can."

"Bossy."

"She really, really wants us to win the tournament."

"Winning isn't the most important thing," said Pearl's mother. "You both know that, don't you?"

"We know," Cody and Pearl sang in chorus.

Cody leaned back. She slid down between the twins. They sucked their thumbs. They made contented, snuffling sounds. Peaceful, not a care in the world—that was the life of a baby. If you were a baby, you didn't worry if your friend still liked you. You didn't even know what a friend was. Or soccer. Or winning and losing. You just expected everybody to love you, and they did.

Cody stared at her orange, zebra-striped feet. She tried to remember being a baby. Very quietly she said, "Goo goo. Gaa gaa."

"No baby talk," said Pearl without turning around. "We speak to the twins in full sentences."

Thus ended that conversation.

10
Exploding House

Cody sat on her bed and tried to re-mend her jacket.

If you think poking bendy thread through a practically invisible hole is easy, you probably never tried it.

Gremlin watched with eyes of encouragement. At last, Cody threaded the needle. She started to stitch.

Something you should know about thread: it loves to tangle up in knots.

Gremlin was always proud of Cody. But tonight, he looked worried. Like maybe, possibly, the hole was still there. Only now it looked even worse.

"Grr." Cody threw the jacket down. She stared at the tree out her window. A little bird flew up and sat on a branch. A bread crust was in its beak.

"Hey!" said Cody. "That was supposed to be for the ants."

"Who are you talking to?" Wyatt stuck his head into the room.

"A robber."

Wyatt picked up her jacket and shook his head. He sat down, snipped away the tangled mess she'd made, and began to stitch.

"I didn't know you could sew!"

"I'm going to be a brain surgeon, remember? I'll do a lot of sewing."

Sticking a needle into a brain! Cody and Gremlin fell over in a greenish faint.

"I hope you know this is futile," said Wyatt.

"Uh-huh." *Futile* must mean "hard but worth it." Cody watched her big brother sew. What would she do without him? "Wyatt? Remember when I wasn't born yet? I bet you were so miserable and lonesome, right?"

Stitch-stitch.

"I bet every time you got to make a wish, you wished for me. On every star and every candle. Right?"

Stitch-stitch.

"Right?"

"Actually I wished for a Jack Russell terrier. But Mom and Dad said I was allergic, so they had to get a baby instead."

Wyatt held up her jacket. The hole had vanished! Cody threw her arms around her big brother.

"You're a genius!" she said.

Houdini headlock time.

Bidda-la-beep! Wyatt released Cody and looked at his phone.

"Payton's coming over to do homework," he said.

Cody followed him down the hall. He took off his T-shirt. He put on his collar shirt and buttoned it up. His eyes bulged.

"You know that monster Big Hands? It's like he's got me by the throat." He shook his head. His hair didn't move. "Don't ask me how people wear *ties*."

Cody wrapped her hands around her neck and did the Frozen Scream. Wyatt laughed and did it, too.

"Tell P.U. you like T-shirts better," said Cody.

"I can't. She's my girlfriend."

"Do you tell her what to wear?"

"Are you insane?"

"When you're on a team, it's supposed to be *we*, not *me*."

Wyatt looked at her.

"Huh," he said. "Sometimes you're almost as good as a Jack Russell terrier." He scratched her behind the ear.

• • •

On Sunday afternoon, Cody walked to Spencer's house. She couldn't wait to work on the museum. She wanted to make a café. And a gift shop. Those were two of her favorite parts of museums.

As she walked, she took big lungfuls of air. It tasted cool and fresh as peppermint candy. Those yellow flowers shaped like trumpets were everywhere. *Make way for the kingdom of spring!* they trumpeted.

If only she could stop worrying about the tournament. It was next weekend. The soccer table talked about it nonstop. Pearl had chewed up all her erasers. Mom was taking Saturday off. Dad was coming, too. Even Wyatt said he'd be there.

Winning is not the most important thing, she told herself.

Oh, yes, it is, argued a voice inside her.

Not.

Is.

Not.

Is.

The tournament was giving Cody the whim-whams. She tried not to think about it.

In this life, trying not to do something can be harder than doing it.

When GG answered the door, she was holding a wooden spoon.

"Just in time for soup!" she said.

GG was playing Cody's favorite Jackson Five album. They moonwalked down the hall to the kitchen, where a big pot simmered on the stove.

"It's my own recipe," she said. "I call it Bundle of Joy soup. I'm trying to tempt Spencer's mama's appetite."

GG gave Cody a taste. A little more salt, they decided.

"Where's Spencer?" asked Cody.

"He and his parents went to look at a house."

That didn't sound very interesting.

"They should be back before too long," said GG. "How about some tai chi?"

GG turned off the Jackson Five and put on her peaceful, wobbly-flute music. They breathed deeply. Slowly and gracefully, they raised their arms.

Whoosh. A stack of papers slid to the floor.

They tried again. Slowly and gracefully, they raised their knees.

Clunk. Cody knocked over Mr. Pickett's golf clubs.

"It's hard to go with the flow when you can hardly
turn around." GG sighed.

"Where are you going to fit the baby?" Cody
asked. "And all the diapers?"

"Pumpkin, if we added a baby to this house, it might explode."

If they added a baby? Cody picked up MewMew. She rubbed the spot that switched on her purring motor.

"I'm going to miss them like crazy cakes." GG sighed again. "But they're right. It's time to get their own place."

Wait. Cody stopped MewMew's head rub. It was possible she stopped breathing, too.

"Their own place?" she repeated. "What do you mean?"

GG's eyebrows did a backbend.

"Didn't Spencer tell you? He and his parents are going to move."

11
Alien Ice Planet

Cody tried to shake her head, but it was frozen on her neck.

"They've been looking at houses every Sunday. They want to be in their own place before the baby comes."

MewMew batted Cody's hand with her paw. This was cat for "More head rubbing, please." But Cody's hand was frozen solid, too.

"The real-estate agent has been taking them all over. It's not easy to find the right place."

Cody had turned into an alien on the Ice Planet.

"Oh, pumpkin." GG made a face of I'm-so-sorry. "Spencer should have told you himself."

GG was a world champion hugger. But even she could not unfreeze Cody.

"Don't you worry," GG said. "You two are friends for life. Nothing can change that."

A friend for life would have told her he had to move. He would have asked her to make a plan. Together, they would have figured out something. Maybe they could build a new room onto GG's house. Or keep the baby in the museum. Or maybe Cody's parents would let Spencer come live with her. Or . . . something.

But did he tell her? No. He kept it a secret. Maybe he was going to move away without a word. In the middle of the night. Without a trace.

Just like the ants. Her other ex-friends.

Cody set MewMew down. GG tried to get her to eat some Bundle of Joy soup, but Cody said no, thank you. She pulled on her apple-red jacket.

In the backyard, Maxie was waving her pom-poms. Molly was trying to rip a tree out of the ground.

"I'm stretching," she said.

"Give me a *K*!" Maxie yelled. "Give me a *O*. Give me a *D*. Give me a *E*. What do you got? Cody!"

Molly released the poor tree. "Want to come for a run with me?"

Run? Cody could barely walk. She was like a clump of old leaves, heavy and soggy.

"Just around the block," said Molly. "But first, a word of advice. Don't try to keep up with me. You'll only collapse in agony."

Cody took off her apple-red jacket. She folded it carefully and set it on the back steps.

They started down the sidewalk. Molly was fast, but not too fast. Cody's shoes hit the sidewalk. Running was so easy, compared to soccer. No balls.

No rules. No win and lose. Just your feet, *thud-thud*. And your heart, *thump-thump*.

They ran all the way around the block. As they passed the house, Maxie shook her pom-poms.

"Stomp!" She stomped. "Scream." She screamed. "For the Molly and Cody team!"

The spring breeze tickled. The bright sun smiled. A cloud shaped like a Hercules beetle floated overhead. Cody's heart *thump-thumped*. Her legs grew lighter.

Back around the corner. Cody could see Maxie trying a cartwheel and falling on her bungie.

She could see the big car pulling into the driveway.

And the Picketts climbing out.

And Mr. Pickett shaking a lady's hand.

And Mrs. Pickett giving Spencer a big, happy hug.

Cody turned and began running in the opposite direction.

"Where are you going?" called Molly, but Cody didn't stop.

. . .

At home, she lay on her belly beside the deserted ant colony.

Then she lay on her back and looked up at the empty sky.

Belly, back. Belly, back.

"Cody!" called Dad. "Phone for you."

Cody jumped up. When Spencer said he was sorry, she'd tell him how he hurt her feelings. When he said sorry again, she'd tell him this wasn't how friends behaved. When he said sorry again, she'd say okay. They would make up. And make a plan so he would not have to move.

"Hello?"

"You need to wear red and black tomorrow."

Pearl.

"We're wearing team colors all week," she said. "Because of the tournament."

Cody leaned against the wall. She slid down to the floor.

"Cody? Are you there?"

Cody nodded. "I mean, yes."

"Madison says it will bring us luck."

"You are under her spell."

Pearl went silent.

So did Cody.

It turned into a war of silence. Who would speak first?

Finally, Cody surrendered.

"I know a new cheer," she said. "Stomp. Scream. For the world's best soccer team."

"Red and black. Madison says if we forget, we'll be in a world of trouble."

"That big boss."

"Good-bye."

Cody waited all night for the phone to ring again. But the only person who called was a man who wanted to know if they had a dry basement.

Before bed, Cody laid out a pair of black pants. She could wear them with her apple-red jacket.

Oh, no. Her jacket! She'd left it on the back steps! There was no telling what those Meens would do with it. Mr. Meen might use it to clean dead bugs off his steel-toed boot. Molly might make it into a pirate flag.

No jacket.

No Spencer.

No Pearl.

No ants.

A world of trouble. That's where she lived right now.

12
Teeter-Totter

Cody didn't mean to be a traitor. But the next morning, she had no choice. She had to wear her new reversible jacket. She chose midnight-blue-cat-side out.

She just couldn't help it.

Spencer waited on the corner. Cody's insides were a teeter-totter. Up, she was happy as ever to see him. Down, she would never forgive him. Up. Down. Up. Down. Up . . .

"Why didn't you tell me?" she burst out. "Some friend you are!"

Spencer's face squished up. For a second, Cody was sure he would cry. Oh! She hated when someone cried. Especially when that someone used to be her best friend for life.

Spencer tugged his woolly hat. He crossed his arms. His face un-squished.

"I'm walking to school by myself," he said, and marched away.

Cody could not believe it. She ran after him.

"You're not allowed! We have to stay together at all times. That's a Non-Negotiable rule."

Spencer kept marching.

"Fine! Go ahead! I don't care! Look at me. La, la, la! Do I look like I care?"

March-march.

Cody's fingers itched to pull that dumb winter hat right off his head and . . . oops!

Spencer spun around. "Give me back my hat."

"Here. And for your information, winter is over!"

March-march.

"It's spring!" she said to his back. "Wearing a winter hat is dumb."

"*Dumb* is not a nice word."

"Dumb dumb dumb!"

He kept right on marching, across the playground and to the school door, where he stood with his arms folded.

"You are not wearing team colors."

Cody spun around. The world was a blur of red and black. Pearl and Madison were covered in it, head to toe. Even their sneakers had one red lace and one black one each.

"I was going to," Cody said. "But I forgot my jacket and . . . "

"Never mind. I made these for all team members." Madison handed her a barrette with red and black ribbons. And then she sneezed.

Cody was not big on ribbons and bows. But she clipped the barrette in her hair.

"Be sure to wear it every day," Madison said. And then she sneezed again. She scowled and turned to Pearl. "I better not be getting your cold," she warned.

"I sanitized constantly," said Pearl.

"Whenever I get a cold, it turns into strep." Madison clutched the neck of her red-and-black sweatshirt. "I cannot get sick. Not with the tournament this weekend. I. Can. Not."

Madison staggered away, and Pearl ran after her. But suddenly she turned around and ran back.

"I love your new jacket," she said. "The cats are so cute."

Pearl couldn't help being nice. Even after she turned into your un-friend, she couldn't help it.

"Thank you," said Cody. "I like it, too, but I miss my old one."

"Like that song. Make new friends, but keep the old."

"Exactly!"

Cody smiled. Pearl smiled. Smile twins, that's what they were.

"That would make a perfect cheerleader barrette," said a small voice.

Cody looked down. What in the world? Maxie was wearing the apple-red jacket. It came to her knees. Another Maxie or two could fit inside.

"For your information," said Cody, "that is my jacket."

"Molly said it's too small for you. She said you don't want it anymore." Maxie flapped the sleeves like wings. "Red's my best favorite. And I love pockets. Soon it'll fit me. Before you know it, I'll be big as you."

She spun around. She stomped her feet. "Give me a *F*. Give me a *R*. Give me a *E*. Give me a . . . a . . . *Z*! What do you have?"

Pearl and Cody looked at each other. "Frez?" they guessed.

"No, silly. Friends!"

"Pearl!" called the Big Boss. "You—" *A-choo!* "You said you'd help me with these barrettes!"

"Coming!" Pearl ran.

"Can I have your barrette?" Maxie asked.

"I wish," said Cody. "But I have to wear it."

"You have to?" Maxie blew a breath. "When I get big as you, I'm doing whatever I want."

・・・

At practice, Coach Y! explained the tournament. Every time you won, you advanced to the next level. If you kept winning, you made the semis.

"Then the finals!" Madison pumped her first. "To the top!"

All at once she started coughing. Her eyes watered. Her face turned pale. Coach Y! patted her on the back.

"Mad, you need to take it easy. Sit down. Have some water."

"I'm okay!" *Cough-cough.* "Soccer is not for weaklings!"

Cody and Spencer were not on speaking terms. They walked to school in single file. After school, Spencer stayed in his room while Cody tried to teach MewMew cat sign language. Every day, she ran around the block with Molly.

"I have to admit, you're not bad," Molly said. "Maybe you can be a track star, too."

Cody pictured herself in a bright-orange track suit. The mayor hung a gold medal around her neck. The crowd cheered. She waved and smiled. A reporter took her picture and said it must feel so wonderful to be World Champion.

Even though winning was not the most important thing.

As they ran back around the corner, she saw Spencer crawl out of the museum. Why was he working on it when he was about to move away?

When Spencer went inside his house, Cody crawled under the porch. Spencer had been busy as a worker ant. There were many new exhibits:

A photo of him and Cody at the winter concert

His leaf project, which the Spindle gave a check-plus-plus *(Cody had found the three different kinds of sassafras leaves)*

A jar of meat tenderizer, from when Cody got stung by yellow jackets

A sign saying REWARD, NO QUESTIONS ASKED, *from when Wyatt's bike got stolen.*

Each exhibit made her remember something they did together. Something fun. Or exciting. A time they stuck up for each other, or taught each other something new. It was a stroll down Memory Lane, and it made Cody overflow with happiness.

But little by little, the happiness leaked out of her. Because Spencer was moving away. Who wanted to remember how things used to be? A Museum of Sadness, that's what he was making. Plus, who knew he'd saved all this stuff? He never told her.

That Spencer! He kept too many secrets. She couldn't trust him anymore.

Cody grabbed a card. She found a red crayon. Red, the color of furious.

I am glad you are moving away. Who wants a friend that is sneaky? I feel sorry for the poor inosent baby that gets you for a brother.

She taped the card to the wall. Wait till he saw that! He'd be sorry he was leaving her in the dust.

13
To Be a Tree

In this life, some things never change:

C-A-T (always spells cat)

Tattoos (always cool)

A tiny monkey (your parents will always say you cannot get one for a pet)

But other things do.

For example, feelings. They can change without warning.

When Cody woke up the next day, she remembered the red-crayon card. *Wrong.* The word lit up inside her brain.

Spencer was sneaky. That was a fact.

But writing that part about the baby was wrong.

That part was plain mean.

She had to tell him sorry. This would be tricky, since they weren't speaking to each other.

But she had to do it.

Cody saved her toast crusts and carried them outside. When you get the habit of feeding something, it is hard to stop.

"I hope you like strawberry jam," she called to the bird perched up in the tree.

The morning air was golden and sweet. If you could eat it, it would taste like butterscotch. Mother Nature was in an excellent mood. In Cody's opinion, this was rude. It was a cloudy, thunderstorm type of day, if you asked her.

She marched to the corner.

No Spencer. A piece of paper lay on the sidewalk.

It said:

In a hurry.

Cody got angry all over again.

"Fine!" she yelled. "Be like that! See if I ever tell you sorry, you Sneaky Pete, you!"

"Are you all right, sweetheart?" An old woman walking her dog looked at her with eyes of worry.

Cody's face turned flaming hot. She gave the dog a pat, then ran all the way to school.

Where the next bad thing happened. She had forgotten her soccer team barrette.

In the classroom, she quick-quick got red and black construction paper. She cut long strips and taped them to her shirt. Just in time. Here came the B.B. Cody held her breath.

But Madison didn't even look at her. She went right to her desk and plonked her head down.

Probably she was saving up her strength for tomorrow.

• • •

That night, Cody did everything Coach Y! had told them. She set out her soccer uniform. She ate a healthy dinner. She went to bed early, to get a good night's rest.

But she couldn't sleep a wink. Toss, turn. Toss, turn.

"Little Seed? Everything okay?" Dad sat on the edge of her bed. He smoothed her hair with his big, strong hand that could steer a big rig. "Are you worried about the tournament?"

"Uh-huh."

"Just remember, the most important thing isn't—"

"But I'm more worried about Spencer!" Cody sat up. "We had a fight. And we didn't make up. What if he moves away and never speaks to me again as long as he lives?"

Another good thing about Dad was he didn't always say what you expected. Now he made eyes of let-me-think. He rubbed his chin. He gazed out the window. At last, he pointed at the tree.

"Remember how cold it was this winter? Remember how our tree got bent down with snow and ice?"

"Uh-huh." Cody remembered. "Sometimes it tapped on my window, and I felt sorry for it."

"But trees are smart. Even on the coldest days,

they know that winter won't last forever. They know spring will come again."

"And now it did!" Cody cried.

"That's right. And know what? Friends go through ice storms and blizzards, too. They have rough and tough times. But they need to wait it out. Because for true friends, just like trees, guess what? Spring always comes again."

Dad tucked her in. He gave her and Gremlin good-night kisses. When Cody drifted off to sleep, she dreamed she was a tree. Birds nested in her leafy branches. They laid speckled eggs, and naked little babies popped out. The babies sang songs of joy.

14
Sudden Death

Cody stared out the car window. This was it. They were on their way to the tournament. Dad tried to lead a sing-along, but Cody's mouth was too dry. It was the Sahara in there.

"You're not nervous, are you?" Mom asked.

"Gaa," Cody croaked. If only she really was a tree. Being a tree was much less complicated than being a human.

"Just do your best. That's all that counts. It's not whether you win or lose that—"

"I know that, Mom!"

Cody sucked on her water bottle. What if she ran the wrong way, or passed to the wrong team, or touched the ball with her hand, or did offsides, which who knew what that was anyway? Everyone would see her mess up.

A voice inside her said, *No they won't. Because all eyes will be on Madison.*

Cody started to relax. Coach Y! was fierce about teamwork, but everyone knew it was really up to Madison. She was the star. She could win the game single-handed. Cody began to feel better.

Till they got to the field. Pearl was pale as the undead.

"Madison has strep. She can't play!"

"Oh, no!"

Everybody was super-epic-wicked worried. Except Coach Y! She called a huddle.

"We are a team," she said. "A mighty, mighty team. We're going to go out there and play our game!"

"But, Coach," Pearl said, "who's going to take Madison's place?"

"All of you. Let me hear it!"

"*We*, not *me*."

They sounded like frogs at the bottom of a deep well. Coach Y! made them say it like they believed it.

"*WE, NOT ME!*"

"Not me, all right." Pearl looked at Cody with eyes of doom. "I'm awful."

"No, you're not."

"Madison said—"

"You're not as good as Madison," Cody interrupted. "Nobody is. But just because you're not the best doesn't mean you're bad."

"Yes, I am."

"Fine. You're bad. Actually, you're stinky rotten no-good terrible!"

Pearl's eyes widened. "No, I'm not!"

"See? I told you."

"Are we ready, team?" cried their coach.

The other team was gold-and-white. This was good. It was easy to tell which team was which. Also, many of them wore looks of I'm-not-exactly-sure-about-this. Maybe they'd never played a tournament before, either.

A tiny seed of hope began to grow inside Cody.

Whee! The ref blew her whistle and the game began.

Ka-pow. Gold-and-white scored.

Ka-pow the Sequel. They scored again.

The seed of hope shriveled up. Without Madison, their team was a disaster. Two girls looked ready to cry. A boy got a stomachache and had to sit down.

"Come on!" yelled somebody's father. "Get it together!"

This was not what you'd call helpful.

Just then, Cody saw Wyatt and Payton ride up on their bikes. Wyatt jumped off and pointed at his chest. What do you know! Instead of a collar shirt, he wore his favorite I ♥ BLOOD AND GUTS T-shirt. Payton didn't look as if she minded. She was smiling her shiny lip-gloss smile. Both of them waved.

Cody waved back.

Just as a ball bonked her in the head.

Where did that come from?

"Go, number six!" yelled Mom.

Ball at her feet. Pearl down the field. No one nearby.

"Pearl!" Cody yelled. "Heads up!"

She focused. She took aim. She put her left foot to that ball and . . .

Right on target! Pearl stared at the ball. For a long moment, she did the Statue.

"Go!" hollered Cody. "Go, Pearl!"

Pearl lurched to life. She hooked the ball and began to dribble. *Dribble-dribble.* She wasn't very good, but good enough. She moved the ball down the field.

A gold-and-white closed in on her, but Pearl put her arms out, just like Coach Y! had taught them. *Dribble-dribble . . .*

"Shoot!" Cody raced up beside her. "Shoot, Pearl!"

Pearl made a face of who-me?

"Yes, you!" said Cody. "You can do it!"

Pearl did.

"Goooooal!"

The crowd went wild.

"That's more like it!" yelled the loudmouth father.

After that, something supernatural happened. It was like their team woke up and discovered they had hidden powers. The defenders started defending. The strikers started striking. The boy with the stomach-ache got better and stole the ball from a gold-and-white. He raced down the field. He zigged. He zagged.

"Goooooal!"

The score was tied. The team ran around doing fist bumps. Nobody could believe it. Yes, they could. They were mighty! They were playing their game!

So was the gold-and-white. They didn't score another goal. But they didn't let Cody's team score one, either. Too soon, the game was over. It was 2–2. A tie.

Uh-oh.

Coach Y! called a huddle.

"We're going into overtime," she told the team.

"Wait," said Cody. "Is that the same as sudden death?"

Coach Y! nodded.

15
Not the Most
Important Thing, Part 2

"We'll play an extra ten minutes," their coach explained. "First team to score during that time wins. Are we ready?"

"Yes."

"Team! I said, are we ready?"

"YES!"

Back on the field, the gold-and-white looked ready, too. The air flashed and fizzed like Fourth of

July sparklers. All the parents were cheering. Payton was jumping up and down. The twins waved their bananas.

Out of the blue, in the middle of everything, Cody thought of Spencer. If only he was here, too, cheering in his careful, Spencer-like way. For a second, she thought she heard him.

Go, Cody! he called. *Do your best! Just don't get bonked in the head with the ball!*

Whee! The ref blew her whistle. The game was on.

Back and forth went the ball, red-and-black, gold-and-white, red-and-black, gold-and-white. Both teams played with all their might.

In this life, time can stand still. Clocks do not move. Ten minutes last forever. Cody's teammates began to get tired. The stomachache boy tried to kick the ball and missed. Pearl tripped and landed on her bungie. When she got up, she wore a look of where-am-I? Somebody got a penalty, for something.

"Get your heads in the game!" the extremely unhelpful father yelled.

Red-and-black did their best, but everyone had tired legs. It wasn't sudden death. It was very slow dying.

Cody was the only one with energy left. The ball went out of bounds, and the gold-and-white did a throw-in. It landed near Cody, but a gold-and-white hooked it and started down the field.

"Stay with her, Cody," called Coach Y!

Thump-thump (Cody's heart). *Clomp-clomp* (her orange cleats). Up the field she raced, chasing the girl with the ball. She narrowed her eyes. She set her jaw. All around her, the rest of the world turned into a blur. She had to get that ball. Had to get it, had to get it, had to . . .

Whoa.

The world went even blurrier. Then it turned completely green.

Grass. Cody and the grass were face-to-face.

"Goooooal!"

She raised her head. All around her, alien cleats jumped for joy. She put her head back down.

Dead. Her team was suddenly dead.

"Cody?" Pearl crouched beside her. "Are you okay?"

"We lost."

"But are you okay?"

Coach Y! ran over. "Cody! Sit up, can you?"

Right behind her was Dad. And Mom. And Wyatt and Payton. Everyone gazed down at her with eyes of worry and love. To tell the truth, this felt kind of nice. Cody lay there an extra second, then sat up.

"I'm okay. But what happened?"

"You were going like the wind," said Payton.

"Their forward came right at you, but you didn't stop," said Dad.

"Till your feet got tangled up," said Mom.

"You did the world's most awesome face-plant," said Wyatt. "But you almost had her!"

"You gave it everything you had," said Coach Y! "And then you gave it some more."

"The heart of a champion," said Pearl. "That's what you have."

Afterward, their team played something called a consolation game. The other team had lost, too. Nobody but nobody was going on to the next level.

You might think this would be depressing.

Instead, it turned out to be fun.

"Pressure's off," said Coach Y! "Let's just enjoy ourselves."

Pearl and Cody sat side by side on the bench.

"Madison would super hate this," said Pearl.

"Wicked epic hate it," said Cody.

They sucked their water bottles.

"Good thing she's not here," said Pearl.

They slid their eyes at each other and did twin smiles.

"But I hope she gets better very soon," added Pearl.

"Right. Me too," said Cody.

Everyone got a small trophy of a player about to *ka-pow* a soccer ball. Coach Y! told them they had played beyond her wildest expectations. She told them they were a true team. They did their cheer one more time.

And then, at last, it was time to go home.

As they drove past Spencer's house, Cody saw him sitting on the porch swing. She asked Mom to stop so she could get out.

When he saw her, Spencer brought the swing to a halt.

"Did you come to my tournament?" asked Cody.

"No."

"Are you sure? I heard your voice."

"Did you get bonked in the head with a ball?" asked Spencer.

"Yes."

"Maybe you were having a hallucination."

Cody sat down on the swing. Usually, she liked to swing fast. Spencer liked to go slow. But now they didn't make it go at all. They hung there in suspended animation.

"Did you win?" asked Spencer.

"Nope."

"Maybe next time."

They were speaking. Cody hoped Spencer didn't notice.

MewMew jumped up and nestled between them. Cody rubbed her switch, and she began to purr. The air vibrated with furry happiness.

Purr-purr. Sniffle-sniffle.

Cody looked at Spencer. His nose was running.

"Uh-oh," she said. "The rhinovirus got you, too."

But Spencer shook his head. His nice round head, which for the very first time did not wear a winter hat. Cody looked closer. Tears shone in his eyes.

"I'm going to miss MewMew so much," he said.

Oh!

"And GG. And this swing. And this porch. And . . . everything."

Oh! Oh! Spencer was crying. Cody leaned so close, she saw herself reflected in his glasses.

"We can still make a plan," she said. "We can figure something out, I know it! You can't move. You . . ."

"See? That's why I didn't tell you."

"What?"

"I tried to. But every time, the words got too scared to come out."

"Scared of what?"

"You!"

Cody sat back so fast her head plonked the swing.

"Me?" She spoke in a voice of quiet. "I'm not scary."

"Yes, you are. Sometimes. You get all . . . what's that word you keep using?" Spencer bared his teeth and narrowed his eyes. He curled his hands into claws.

"Fierce?"

"Uh-huh. I knew you'd get upset and say I couldn't move." Spencer dug his fist into his cheek. This was not a fun thing to watch. "But I have to go. I'd miss my parents too much. And the new baby needs me. It doesn't have any downloads, remember?"

Cody rubbed her plonked head. Her thoughts spun round and round. Spencer hated things to change. Even tiny things. A new baby plus a new house? It might as well be an earthquake. His whole world was smithereened.

But he was right. He had to move. Cody had been so sad for herself, she'd forgotten to think how he felt.

Maybe it wasn't too late to try.

"Is your new house nice?" she asked.

"I have to sleep in a room that's way bigger. With two windows instead of one."

"You'll have lots of space for your LEGOs."

"That's what my parents say." He did some blinking. "They say I can get a pet."

"Ask for a tiny monkey!"

"I'm going to get tropical fish."

"Oh." Cody tried again. "Maybe I can come visit you. I'll ask my parents to drive me."

"You don't have to drive. You can just run."

"Ha, ha. I'm good at running, but I can't run for miles and miles."

"You can run four blocks. I saw you and Molly and—"

"Wait. What?" Cody jumped off the swing. "Do you mean to tell me you're only moving four blocks away?"

"*Only?* Everything will be different. The front door is red. I'm used to a plain door. And . . ."

Cody threw herself onto the swing. Her heart was a spring day, budding and blooming.

"Everything will be changed," she said. "But the most important things will stay just the same."

"That doesn't make sense."

Yes, it did. But Cody didn't try to argue. She was

too happy. Besides, it was no use. If you enjoyed arguing with a tree, you would enjoy arguing with good old, trusty, best friend for life Spencer.

Cody started to swing. Slowly at first, then a little faster. MewMew purred. Spencer stopped sniffling. In the ruffly bush beside the porch, a bird sang a song of joy. In the distance, another one did an echo. That was bird for "It was a long, hard winter, but hooray! Spring has come to us again!"

16
The Museum of . . .

Mr. and Mrs. Pickett were packing up the moving van. Everyone was helping. GG. Mom. Dad. Wyatt. Mr. Meen. Molly and Maxie.

MewMew's job was to jump in and out of the boxes and suitcases.

"She's the inspector," said GG. She poured them all more lemonade. Moving was hard work, and everyone was hot and thirsty. By now, it was hard to remember a little thing called winter.

Cody carefully carried out a box marked DISHES.

"Cody, you are such an enormous help." Mrs. Pickett smiled. Her barfing days were over. By now, you could tell there was a baby in there, all right.

After a while, Cody sat on the swing for a rest. She looked around. That was when she noticed that Spencer had disappeared.

Thump-thump. The porch floor vibrated under her feet. She jumped down the steps and crawled into the museum. Spencer was writing on a piece of poster board.

"What are you doing?"

He held up a wait-a-minute finger.

Cody sat on the rug and looked around. They never got a chance to make the gift shop or café. They never even got a chance to give the museum a name. Now, she realized, Spencer would pack it up and take it with him.

Cody tucked her knees under her chin. She folded herself up tight. She was a seed in the ground. One that would never get to bloom.

Spencer kept writing. He was making every single letter perfect-perfect.

"What is so important?" she asked.

Up went that annoying finger again.

Cody kicked off her flip-flops. She wriggled her bare toes in the warm dirt. Overhead, footsteps went back and forth. Maxie sang "100 Bottles of Beer on the Wall" till Molly told her she had to stop. Wyatt's phone did its *bidda-la-beep,* and he gave a mush-brained laugh.

"Spencer, I cannot wait one more second."

At last he turned around. "Can you help me hang this up?"

"I hate to tell you"—Cody did a breath—"but it's time to pack up, not hang up."

He showed her the poster board. Every letter was

a different color. Every letter was perfect-perfect. It
said:

The Museum of Friends

Cody read it. She read it again.

"Wait," she said. "That's what kind of museum it is?"

Spencer nodded. "The museum of you and me."

Cody looked around at the many wonderful exhibits. It was true.

"I didn't want you to be sad after I moved," he said. "So I made it for you."

In this life, sometimes you feel so many different feelings at once, your heart can't tell what is going on.

Together, they hung up the sign near the museum entrance. Sitting side by side, they gazed around at the exhibits.

"We did a lot of cool stuff," Spencer said.

"I know," Cody said. "And we'll do lots more."

The Museum of Friends! She prickled all over with happiness. Her head. Her heart. Her belly. Even her feet.

Wait. That wasn't happiness prickling her toes.

Ants! A long parade of them. They marched over the rug and skedaddled across her toes.

"Look," she cried. "Museum ants!"

Overhead, footsteps crisscrossed the porch. Cody and Spencer heard steel-toed boots, designer sandals, track shoes, and high-tops. They listened to voices laughing and talking and grunting.

"Where did that Spencer go?" they heard his mother ask.

"And that Cody," her mother added. "Where are those two, anyway?"

Spencer and Cody grinned but didn't make a sound. Soon they'd crawl back out. Soon they'd join everyone up there in the bright, busy, blooming world.

But not yet. For now, they wanted to think about all the stuff they'd done together. And all the stuff they'd still do. They wanted to think about the things that had changed. And the things that never, ever, as long as they lived, would.

So they stayed a little longer. Just the two of them. And the ants.

From the first day of summer vacation all the way through fall and winter to long-awaited spring, there's a full year of adventure for Cody and her neighbors!

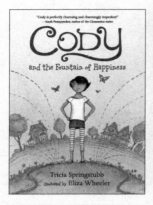

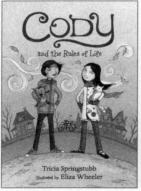

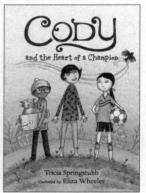

"Springstubb creates a kind of magic in these books, with their gentle humor . . . and real empathy for kids struggling to figure out how to do the right thing."
—*The Buffalo News*

www.candlewick.com